I0633800

Nothing Resplendent Lives Here

STORIES

Renuka Raghavan

Červená Barva Press
Somerville, Massachusetts

Copyright © 2022 by Renuka Raghavan

All rights reserved. No part of this book may be reproduced in any manner without written consent except for the quotation of short passages used inside of an article, criticism, or review.

Červená Barva Press
P.O. Box 440357
W. Somerville, MA 02144-3222

www.cervenabarvapress.com

Bookstore: www.thelostbookshelf.com

Cover photo: Renuka Raghavan

Cover design: William J. Kelle

ISBN: 978-1-950063-71-0

Library of Congress Control Number: 2022932381

ACKNOWLEDGMENTS

Many thanks to the editors of the following journals where these stories were first published, some in early forms:

Bending Genres: "Chestnut Street"
Boston Literary Magazine: "Rebound"
Bright Flash Literary Review: "God Maker"
Flash Boulevard: "Self-Helped" and "Extinct"
Nixes Mate, Climate Change Issue 21/22: "Looking for Sagittarius"
Pensive: A Global Journal of Spirituality and the Arts: "Event Horizon"
South Florida Poetry Journal: "Fur Babies"
Spirit's Tincture: "Writing Material"
The American Journal of Poetry: "Scab"
The Beechwood Review: "Hazards of Jesting"
The Drabble: "Coyotes" and "Fulcrum"
Unlikely Stories Mark V: "Hurdles"

I remain indebted to my nurturing writing community of teachers, mentors, peers, and other fellow artists who have conversed, bolstered, and encouraged me along the way.

To Červená Barva Press, especially Gloria Mindock, thank you for believing in my work. Thank you, Karen Friedland, Eileen Cleary, Christine Jones, Rich Feinberg, Francine Witte, Jayne Martin, and Robin Stratton.

Finally, eternal gratitude to my loving family. Thank you for rooting me in unconditional strength, love, and support, always.

TABLE OF CONTENTS

I.

II.

III.

For Vijay, Riya, and Raj

Nothing Resplendent Lives Here

Stories

I.

The worst loneliness is to not be comfortable with yourself.
—Mark Twain

Nothing Resplendent Lives Here

People never came to the Oasis because it was a destination, or because it had been their plan all along. It was usually a combination of bad luck and a lack of other options that brought them to me. Most arrived angry, some in tears, and some are so fucked up they have to lean against the wall to pull out their wallets. I treat them all the same, firm but kind. I figure they deserve that much, at least. I smile at the beginning when they check in, and as long as they haven't trashed the room, I smile when they return the key and check out. The porn channel is always an extra fifty dollars.

One morning, around 3 A.M., a man came out of a room on the first floor, shirt half-buttoned, pants unzipped, boots barely on right. He got into his car and sped away, leaving the door to his room wide open. I stood there waiting for someone inside the room to close it, but when that didn't happen, I walked over and peeked in. A naked woman lay on the floor at the foot of the bed. I didn't realize what I was looking at until it was too late.

It was past dawn by the time the police arrived. Their questions hypnotized me, but I was not much help. I walked back to the parking lot since the sun was out, and even though it was useless for warmth during this time of year, I still like the feel of light on my skin. Its gentle pressure keeps me from thinning into nothing, like a single drop of blood lost and diluted in an endless sea.

Fulcrum

The kids made funny faces and gagging sounds at the stuffed cabbage I made for dinner, so I heated up chicken nuggets, instead. Proud in my ability to be more compassionate than my mother had been. What a terrible waste of time all those battles fought over green peas, broccoli, liver, and fish, had been. That time when Mother tried to force mutton into my mouth with her other hand around my neck? Later, that became a humorous anecdote. Whenever there was a lull during a family gathering, that story was told and retold to much cheer and laughter. Funny how no one ever noticed me leaving the room, so claustrophobic with anger and embarrassment that it hurt to breathe.

Extinct

The Stegosaurus display was Andy's favorite at the museum. It wasn't as mainstream and in your face as the T-Rex, he thought. What a show-off. Nor was it as visited as the Triceratops, who, let's face it, was only famous because of that one scene in that dinosaur movie. The Stegosaurus was a calm loner and completely fine with it. You could tell he really wasn't bothered by much.

"You're still here? I was in the bathroom for a while, the line took forever," Andy's wife said, joining him at his side.

"Yeah, I'm still here," Andy sighed. "I really love this fella."

"Well, I want to see all of them. Let's keep walking."

"Look how unbothered he is."

"By 'he' you mean the artificial dinosaur model in front of us?"

"He's just minding his own business, eating leaves, not sweating any of the small stuff. Still died, though. Probably burnt to a crisp right in front of his Stegosaurus wife and kids."

"And on that note, you stay here as long as you want. I'm moving on. See you later, Andy."

Andy wondered if the Steg would have lived just a little bit longer if he'd moved on and chose another patch to graze in when the end came. Maybe, maybe not. Just a victim of circumstance. Poor son of a bitch.

Self-Helped
a story in dialogue

"I need to return these. All of them are overdue, so I need to pay some fines, too. Here's my library card."

"I can certainly help you with that. Let's see here. Do you have *The Secret to Happiness?*"

"No, and the book didn't either. Here it is."

"Oh, I see what you did there! Clever! It's 3 months overdue, so that brings the fine to $13.50 for that one. Do you have *How Bald Guys Can Score Hot Chicks?*"

"Yep. Here you go."

"Okay. 3 months out, so another $13.50 for this one. What about *How to Become the Pope?*"

"It's here."

"Ah, this one is 50 days late, so $7.50. Now then, how about *Anyone Can Be Cool, But Awesome Takes Practice?*"

"Yep, it's right here."

"Looks like this one's been out for 112 days, so that brings the fine to $16.80 for this one. And the last book, *The Joy of Solo Sex?*"

"That one, I lost. I can't find it anywhere."

"Oh dear. For lost books, we have to apply the maximum charge of $24."

"Just as well. What's the total damage?"

"It comes out to $75.30. But…you know, how about you just pay the $24 for the lost book and I can cancel out the rest of the fines. You've returned the books, so no real harm done."

"Really? That's awfully kind of you. Here's the $24. I do appreciate this."

"Oh, don't mention it. Really, please don't mention it, I could get in trouble."

"How about I return the favor? Could I at least buy you a coffee?"

"Oh, uh, I'm not sure. I shouldn't really."

"You know it's not every day a guy like me meets someone as beautiful or as kind as you. Won't you please let me say thanks?"

"Okay. Sure. I just need to finish up here and clock out. Can you wait 10 minutes?"

"You bet! I'll meet you right outside!"

"Hey Brock, it's me. It's me, Kevin. You'll never guess what happened! You remember me checking out those useless self-help books back when you were visiting? Yeah…yeah, those books. You thought I'd lost my damn mind, but what did I say? I said, calm down, I had a reason to check those books out. You remember, Brock? You remember me telling you I had a plan? Well guess what? Those stupid books just landed me a date with a hot librarian. So, who's the fuck-up now?"

Punishment for the Damned

In hindsight, regardless of whatever subconscious post-traumatic reasoning I blamed it on, leaving Dad's ashes in the trunk of my car after his funeral was probably not the best idea. Maybe it was because when he'd introduce me to others, he'd say, "This is my dunce, Charlie." Or maybe it was because no matter what I achieved in my life he was always there to remind me I'd amount to nothing in the end. He used to tell me ghost stories as a kid. Then, after I was asleep, he'd sneak into my room with a sheet over his head and scream bloody murder. I peed my pants more than once, and the whole family nearly died laughing. I guess he was trying to teach me something, but to this day, I sleep with a night light.

When I went down to go to work the morning after his funeral, the trunk was wide open. Some asshole had punched out the lock and pried the trunk open. My spare tire was gone, as was my jack, and the urn containing the ashes. The sun can seem so cruel in a moment like that. The trees, the way they just stand there staring, and every dog in the neighborhood snickering at you. Sometimes your own skin can feel like the worst sort of punishment.

Aberration

I sensed it as soon as I walked into the coffeehouse. Something was off. No one played chess at the window table. A few lone customers sat glumly at the tables meant for two, staring dead into their coffee. No radio playing the local game. No music.

It was probably me. I have this tendency. I'll pick a place, like that bar on the corner of Forsythe and 6th, for example, and stop in for a drink. I'd go every night for months on end, know everyone by name, bartending staff, wait staff, other regulars like me, feel right at home, and then all of a sudden it all turns to rot. Nothing changed, it's the same bar, same seat, same whiskey neat, but out of nowhere the rough, nail-bitten, blood-nicked fingers of the waitress make me retch. The toilet seat covered in bottle caps hanging on the bathroom door like a wreath goes from kitsch to repellent. The pretzels and popcorn feel like gravel in my hands and mouth. I scramble to leave and vow to never go back. I've done this before, to restaurants, libraries, jobs, ex's apartments, just thinking about those places makes me ill.

So I just assumed this was another similar episode when I saw Gayle who I've never known to be anything but cheerful fighting back tears, not even managing to greet anyone. I approached the counter and braced for that wave of inexplicable dread to wash me out onto the street.

Gayle approached sighing heavily, and giving me a half-nod, *Chris passed away last night*, she said. Chris was Gayle's partner and co-owner of the coffee shop. *He went to the hospital in the morning, and he was gone by suppertime. That Covid shit. Gonna have to close when the lockdown starts tomorrow.*

I got a refill, picked up some groceries, and headed home. Something was different, but this time it was the rest of the world. Was it selfish of me to feel absolute relief?

Writing Material

Aparna relished the warmth under the amber glow of spotlight. Grabbing the mic in front of her, she began reciting a story in a unique, rhythmic cadence she was known for. She spoke of the time she slit her wrist at the age of fifteen, and how it differed slightly from the time she tried it again at seventeen. Aparna's prose touched the audience like a mother's caress, soft but perceptible.

Through the crowd of riveted spectators hanging on her every word, Aparna felt *her* there, standing at the very back glaring at Aparna with that panic-inducing stare that had always made her petite stature seem impenetrable. Red glossy lips, pursed in disappointment. Shame. Regret? Long black coconut-oiled hair braided down her back, wrists adorned with gold bangles, stacked to hide her own failed scars; rotund body wrapped in a silk brocaded sari draped in pleats over her left shoulder.

After the reading, the roaring applause, the well-deserved standing ovation, under a deluge of praise, Aparna walked home scurrying through the city's darkness from one streetlight to the next. Aparna asked *her*, then, in the creeping silence that followed the passing city bus, "Does this dress look pretty on me?"

"Your arms are too fat for sleeveless. When will you learn to dress properly? I don't know."

Aparna stopped in the middle of a pedestrian stone bridge staring at the still waters below. "What did you think of my story, Ma?"

"Why didn't you finish your studies with a proper degree? Respectable women don't tell silly stories."

Just as she had when she lit her mother's pyre ablaze one year ago, Aparna forgave her mother's gauche words again. Tonight, over the black water, the moon shone especially bright, illuminating Aparna's dress with an ethereal glow, like a deity who spoke dactylic truths others could not brave.

December

Tonight, the house was so frigid, it pulled itself closer to the ground and the trees just to feel some warmth.

Last week, I stacked a pile of laundry fresh out of the dryer and I dove into it like it was a pile of raked autumn leaves, as if I thought I could stop the fading, as if I could keep the colors alive if I held them in my hands.

Winter arrived and hung around like that spotted owl who patrols my street from the giant oak in my backyard, annoyed at my foolish surprise at his sudden appearance.

When the repairman rang my doorbell this afternoon to service my broken heater, I greeted him in plaid pajama bottoms and an old sweatshirt, cereal bowl in hand, milk dripping down my chin.

Thanks for coming so soon, I exclaimed. *It's been freezing all night, despite using three blankets.* As I led him to the heater, he considered the pile of unfolded laundry and me in my 2pm pajamas. *Is it just you, then*, he asked? *Yep, just me*, I said. *Well, let's make sure you don't freeze tonight*, he said.

It's mid-December, nobody asked if I was ready for winter, but at least someone cared if I was warm.

God Maker

Your watch says half past ten as you look out to the Arabian Sea thinking of a different sunny seashore on the other side of the world, nursing your second gin and tonic at this Mumbai dive bar you overheard a tour guide suggest because it was famous for kebabs, spotting Bollywood stars score cocaine, and meeting one-night stands, when you realize yours is a no-show and you stand to leave but the music starts up and Rihanna swears she found love in a hopeless place and you smile as you light a cigarette because you know the DJ who's been eyeing you all night played the song just for you, then he makes his way over to your table and you smile at him as he grabs your waist and the two of you dance all hot, sweaty, delicious and you just want more, more dancing, more drinks, and later as you lie in the hotel room, DJ tells you he has never left this city, that his whole life is encompassed within one neighborhood, that his biggest fear is to die here without seeing the world, which is probably why he likes to fuck tourists, you realize, then he tells you he comes from a family of god makers, people who make tiny fat Ganesh figures that you've seen hawked on city streets and at crowded intersections all over town, give me your address and I'll mail you one, he says, but all you want to do is tell him you don't have a permanent address, that you have to leave before morning because here the sunrise has a way of emptying everything inside of you.

Welcome, Louisiana

Oh, you want a Christmas story? Yeah, I've got one for you. I was eighteen thumbing my way in and out of trouble down in Louisiana, at the time, when this old boy picked me up in his Cadillac on Christmas Eve right outside a town called Welcome. He asked me if I was hungry. I said, of course I was, and he told me he had a box of beignets in the backseat that I could have. He was a manager at a bakery, see, and he got to take home all the leftovers, all the mistakes, all the ugly ones. He handed me a box of four apple cider beignets, and I dug right into them, eating every last one. He said he'd drop me off at the bus depot in the next town, but before I knew it, he was asking, *And what do I get in return for my generosity, darlin?*

All my years living on the streets, I knew ain't nothing was free. I should've guessed this was coming, but I'm not gonna lie, something about this guy scared me. I got the feeling that he might pull a gun on me if I refused, so instead of answering him, I told him first I needed to pee real bad. He slowed down and pulled over to the side of the road. I was out that door and running as fast as my feet could take me. I crouched down in an overgrown briar patch where I could watch him. Sure enough, he fired a few shots at me from a small handgun he had in his jacket. After a while, he got back in his car and drove off. I didn't much believe in Jesus, but I thanked him all the same right then.

After an hour or so, I started walking again. It was freezing cold, and the wind made it even worse. I must have looked like a right mess; I knew no one would stop to give me a lift. Then, on the side of the road, I saw a blanket. I ran to it, thinking I could use it to warm up, even if it was a little damp. When I lifted it up off the ground, I saw that there was something inside. A possum, I thought, but it was a baby. A tiny pale blue baby. I thought it was dead, but then it started to cry. My first thought was to leave it be and continue down the road, but it was a baby. Alone. On Christmas.

I shoved it up under my top, and I shivered because I shit you not, that baby was as cold as ice. I could feel its heart beating right next to mine. Cars passed, ignoring my waves. That was the first time in my life I prayed for a cop to drive by. I walked for a few miles, and I could feel the baby moving around under my shirt. As I tried to adjust us both, the baby went right for my tit, like I was his mama or something. I started to cry just then feeling completely hopeless, but my tears froze before they could fall.

Then, I saw a small parish church lit up for the holidays on a hill not too far from the road. I climbed over there and banged on the door. A kind Black woman, who was cleaning up from their services earlier that evening, let me in. She took the baby from me, changed its blanket and set about making it comfortable. She rocked the baby and sang hymns while her husband, the pastor, called an ambulance. The sheriff picked me up and gave me an empty cell to sleep in for the night. I appreciated it because even though it was a police station, holiday decorations were all around, even a big Christmas tree. The next day, he gave me a cup of coffee and a present from under the tree, a brand-new coat. It wasn't until he put me on a bus back to New Orleans when he told me the baby didn't make it after all.

The following year I found myself passing through Welcome again, so I went looking for that church since I never did thank the pastor or his wife that night. Only, I never found it again. Some folks said the church burned down, and just like that, it's as if that night never even happened.

II.

The meeting of two personalities is like the contact of two chemical substances: if there is any reaction, both are transformed.
—Carl Jung

Brave Heart

Rohan came home late with the news that Daniel Rubenstein hanged himself in his garage after the firm gave half of his accounts to the younger, new hire. No note, no nothing. He left a wife and three kids, just like that. He doesn't say any more about it after dinner, but I know it weighs heavy on Rohan's mind. He spends the night tossing and turning only to wake up and check his phone for any new work emails.

Anjali calls for me, awake suddenly from a bad dream and I join her in bed, rub her shoulder and hum her back to sleep. A shelf across the room displays my old Care Bear collection, each one a different shade of neon or pastel. The glow of the moon shining through the window lights up Brave Heart Lion's eyes. The colors waltz across the wall and look so real that I have to stand to try and touch it.

By the time I return to our bedroom, Rohan is back in bed, asleep. He moans lightly and turns away from me. His clothes for the next day are already meticulously laid out, shirt, suit, tie, socks, shoes. In the far corner of the room, his old guitar looks on in silence. When we met in college, he played in a rock band. Tomorrow, Anjali and I will ask him to play us a song.

J35

I'm sleeping under the skylight, poorly serenaded by the late afternoon summer storm when he says to me, *Have I ever told you how your eyes remind me of the ocean? You know when it's so blue, it's almost black?* Only, he's looking up at the skylight, too. His hand, slack behind my back, snakes its way to rest on my abdomen. *Jesus, thank God we dodged that bullet, babe,* he says.

Savory aromas from the Italian restaurant across the street creep in through the slightly opened windows. NPR plays on the radio. A killer whale is carrying her dead calf around somewhere off the Pacific Coast. They call her J35. Sometimes she swims by nudging the carcass with her nose, sometimes she grips the dead whale's flipper in her mouth. If the calf drifts away, she dives to retrieve it. It's going on the fifteenth day now.

Fish are so fucking weird, he says. *Orcas are not fish,* I say, folding myself out of his hold.

Event Horizon

After you died, I felt like fucking your pillow before ripping it to shreds, stuffing the feathers into a burrito and eating it with enough Sriracha on it to make my nose run— but it wasn't because I loved you or missed you.

It was because you collected National Geographic magazines since college, and now a small stack of those yellow-bordered books lay under the mail slot covered in dust, the dog's piss, and other domestic detritus I can't be bothered with anymore.

It was because you would quote Pushkin or Gogol whenever I asked you to take out the trash.

It was because every corner of our house is ingratiated with you: your butt print on the corner sofa seat, your coffee mug taunting me from the cupboard, your bathrobe, your pillow.

Your stupidly expensive, down pillow that still smells of you.

It was because our story ended, before it barely began.

It's because I found out it's going to be a girl.

It's because I am just skin and bones now, particles and fragments of my former whole self, orbiting the edges of a black hole, a forced heartache that is intense, distorted, and completely inescapable.

Disclosure

Dad insists that Joey is full of shit when I tell him what Joey said to me last night. I lean in close and speak quietly so no one else in the diner can hear. Dad says men always cast aspersions on rape victims.

"They all do. Cops, priests, even therapists. You should've known better than to tell him," he says.

"Obviously, I thought he'd react differently," I say.

"I'll tell you what. If he ever says anything like that to you again, I'll kill him. Chop his fucking head right off."

"Well, that's nice, Dad. Real lovely."

It's the alcohol. It makes him hostile sometimes. It comes out of nowhere, like the time I invited him to dinner with me and my boss. Dad ended up with his hands around my boss's neck. Luckily, he didn't press charges, but he made it clear he wouldn't be signing any more paychecks either. Yet another job lost. Quite a few of my messes have been because of Dad or other men in my life. I only wish they were man enough to admit it.

Equinox

Marty shops strictly off the grocery list, but I like to go rogue every now and then. So, when he's out of town for a whole week, I hit the Stop & Shop and buy whatever I want: salami, potato chips, French onion dip, boxed macaroni and cheese, two pints of ice cream and two boxes of red wine. The store is getting ready for Easter with pastel rainbows vomited onto every surface and cardboard bunnies peeking out from every corner. Why is it that supermarkets are always celebrating something or another?

Only one checkout lane is open, so I grab a *People* magazine and join the long line. The old man behind me bumps me with his shopping cart. Once. Twice. After the third time, I turn around and say, "Excuse me." He holds out his hands and grimaces apologetically, all eight of his teeth showing. People often think I'm angry when I'm not. Something about me is too hard. Resting Bitch Face, my daughter had diagnosed years back.

The days are getting longer now. There's still a westward orange glow in the sky when I finally emerge from the store. A hippie chick asks me to sign a petition. I refuse, but make sure to smile when I say no. Moths circle the lights peppered throughout the parking lot, heroic in their single-minded, effulgent stupor.

Rebound

Mike died on Friday and by Sunday, Grief arrived like my monthly period, at the worst time possible and not giving a rat's ass what I thought about it. As if that wasn't enough, I could tell he wanted something in return, something good. *Don't lollygag*, he scolded, *I've got other places to go. Your kids, for example.* He stayed like an unwanted guest, that friend of a friend who was never invited but came over nonetheless. Grief became the fly on my wall. And oh, how he loved to play games, Hide and Seek—his favorite—popping up to scare me when I least expected it. God only knows what he'd do to my children. My sweet babies. They stand, inserting quarter after quarter into the Claw machine, *Mama, we're gonna get a new toy.* Grief stood by and watched it all, something he's very good at. In the end, the kids didn't catch the stuffed monkey. I saw Grief snicker and snort even though he tried to hide it. That night, after dinner, Grief lingered as I did the dishes, kids already asleep. *Let's have a drink*, he said. We clinked our wine glasses and slipped into a silent familiarity. After the third round, we staggered upstairs and shed our skins on the bedroom floor.

Beauregard's Final Bloom

Beau showed up on that summer morning sporting a fat lip and his right arm in a sling, but the first thing I noticed when I opened the front door was the giant six-foot urn on my porch, behind him.

"Hi Honey," he greeted, as if he hadn't been away for the past two months. "Look what I brought ya."

"Beauregard Mathison, what the hell have you gone and done now?"

Beau smiled and rubbed the back of his neck with his good hand. "Can I come in? Sure am tired, not to mention, starving."

He came inside, plopped his jacket and duffel bag by the stairs. I made him a bologna sandwich with mustard, olives, and pickles, his favorite. He downed a glass of buttermilk and smiled a sweet smile.

"Talk. What are you doing here, Beau?"

"I missed you, baby. Brought you a surprise, thought it'd cheer you up."

"Is it that humongous urn sitting on my porch? What the hell's in it?"

"You always did love your flowers. Thought I'd bring you the biggest one there ever was."

The unexpected gift distracted me from the urge I had to wring his neck for disappearing on me. For the past few weeks, my only thoughts had been about him. Why had he disappeared? Would he ever return? His sudden presence back in my life made me content, and for now, that's all I wanted.

A quick internet search yielded the answers Beau didn't supply. *Rafflesia arnoldii*, also known as the corpse flower. An endangered species famous for having the largest bloom known to man, four-feet wide, and when fully bloomed it emitted an odor of decaying flesh. The plant was a parasite and needed a host to thrive. That meant we needed to re-plant the thing, and soon. Fuck.

"Where'd you get it?" I asked, hands on hips, like a mother scolding her child. "And how'd you even get that huge thing onto my porch? I never heard anyone pull up."

"Why does any of that matter right now? It's here. And it's all yours."

"It matters because this isn't any regular flower, Beau!"

He smiled that sweet smile again, it always reminded me of my old basset hound, Henry. He'd chew up something he wasn't supposed to and look up at me with regretful eyes. Beau reminded me a lot of Henry. I decided I was exhausted from the day and retired for a nap.

I awoke to warm, wet, suction on my big toe. Figures he'd go for them first, Beau and his damn foot fetish. He worked his way up and soon he was slamming into me with the smoothness of a bucking rodeo horse.

Over the next few weeks our routine was simple but agreeable. We'd spend the morning mostly outside. Beau digging, now that he had use of both arms, readying the ground for the giant flower, while I researched more about it on the internet. When Beau got tired of digging, we'd have lunch, sex, a restful nap, and then cook supper together in the evening. The days became a blur; every moment was Beau-infused, and like him, experiences were fleeting but memorable.

One morning, as Beau ran into town for special soil, I sat on the toilet staring in disbelief at two blue lines on a stick still dripping with urine. I waited for Beau's return, heart thumping in my chest. That's when I realized his duffel bag and jacket were gone.

The flower was never planted. It remained in the urn and the urn remained on my front porch. Neighbors complained it was an eyesore. I didn't care, I didn't want anything to do with it. When it finally bloomed it was hard to tell if the putrid odor was typical for a corpse flower or because it was slowly dying inside the urn.

Zero Gravity

Emily spreads her loot on the coffee table as soon as we return home. Dozens of full-sized candy bars, pretzels, chocolates, even some cash. She claps with glee. I ignore the black duffel bag left by the door.

I knew Richard wouldn't be home when we got back but I hadn't expected the TV to be left on. A muted football game plays in the background. Wherever it's happening, it is snowing. Drifts were forming on the sidelines and flakes were sticking to the camera lens blurring the action on the field. Emily takes her empty pumpkin bucket and bangs it on the table. When I tell her it's time to go up for a bath, she pretends she's an astronaut on her way to the bathroom. She tiptoes around the living room in slow motion, holding her breath, and pretending to float up the stairs.

Ignoring the overwhelming wave of nausea that suddenly sweeps over me, I drag Richard's bag from the entryway onto the sofa to snoop through his forgotten possessions. I put on his college sweatshirt and the pair of socks I gave him last Christmas. At the bottom of the bag, I discover all the unseen years that will never be, wholly entranced by the gold glint of his wedding band.

Searching for Scraps

Good lord, the kid is hysterical again, only this time he is struggling to open the door of my Sentra, as I almost kill us both, veering into oncoming traffic to try and stop him, so I pull into an empty parking lot to calm the kid down, because I know—I get it—he is tired and cranky, and now he won't let me touch him, but the donut place is still lit up, so I tell him if he will behave like a big boy, he can order whatever he wants and he gestures for me to take his hand and lead him inside, and I don't even say a word when he orders more than he could possibly eat, instead I ask the cashier to add a cup of coffee and I pay the bill before we sit across from each other at a table near the window and I ask for a small chunk of his bear claw, but in response, he shoves the pastry back into the paper bag and hugs it close to his chest, and we are left listening to each other sigh as we are serenaded by somber music playing through the speakers and a thick fog settles outside, smearing the lights shining down on the empty lot and I watch seagulls roam about searching for scraps, then I remember that we are less than a mile from the ocean, and that I have come about as far as I can go in this direction.

Lehenga Skirts and Pink Pumps

The parties were always bigger in the old days. You remember those huge raucous family parties we used to have for Diwali? When Avi came up from North Carolina and Mona would come down from Buffalo? The old days when a silent gesture dangled in the air like a promise? Nobody comes around anymore. The holidays are just me and my brother, Dev. You should see him now, eyes all swollen up with cataracts, diabetic and overweight, still stubborn, still single.

Oh, but back when the kids were young, running through the house wearing superhero capes and fairy wings, back before Ashok's heart attack...those were parties. The music, the dancing, the food, the clothes. I still have that lehenga skirt and those matching pink pumps. Remember how Sai always said I had the sexiest midriff? So much effort to make sure everything was just right. And it was all worth it. Then, of course, the kids would make a mess of everything. Remember how I used to get so upset? All that food plastered to the floor like a mosaic fresco.

I would give anything for the kids to be small again and to wake up in the morning and have a cup of chai with Ashok. Anything to go back there. But now the kids all have their own kids and don't come around much. I get to see them maybe once a year, and most years not even around the holidays. It is what happens when everyone moves and gets older, I know. Husbands die and the celebrations get smaller before fading altogether. You spend more and more time alone with nothing but your thoughts. Thinking about what, I'm not even sure anymore.

Hurdles

On her way home from work, Florentina got off the bus and decided to stop at the store. Publix was a four-block walk, so the tiny corner convenience store owned by a Pakistani couple would suffice. It wasn't too bad, despite the store always smelling of rancid meat, at least they always had what she needed. The wife who runs the register is always friendly, unlike her husband who mostly barks orders while stocking inventory. Today, he is out front painting over fresh graffiti and muttering to himself in another language. Florentina waves goodbye on her way out, grocery bag full of milk, bread, chocolate, and tampons.

A young woman holding a baby blocks Florentina's path. She holds out her hand and asks for money, her raspy voice barely above a whisper. Her baby is sick, she explains, and needs medicine. "Please," she begs. "Can you spare anything?"

"Where do you live?" Florentina asks.

The woman looks back, over her shoulder. A boy wearing a black hoodie pokes his head out from behind a tree, watching their exchange. Florentina suddenly remembers her neighbor, Pam, who told her how a girl with a baby came to her door asking for money. The girl said she was starving and going to faint, so Pam let her inside to rest on the sofa while she went to the bathroom to get a pack of diapers and formula she had purchased for her grandson. When she came back, the girl was gone along with Pam's wallet.

Florentina's chest flutters and quakes, like a bird was set loose inside of her. "Sorry," she says. "I don't have anything."

"Please," the woman says. "I'm afraid my baby will die. Anything would help. Just a buck or two?"

"What kind of medicine can you buy for that much?"

As if on cue, the baby screams into the cool night settling around them. Florentina hurries past the woman and the distraught baby. When she reaches the corner, she looks back and sees the woman and the boy staring at her with steely eyes and hard expressions on their faces.

All the sidewalks on Florentina's street are broken and uneven. Slabs are buckling from numerous tree roots pushing up from underneath, looking like jagged teeth protruding from the ground at odd angles. Florentina goes over them faster than she should while carrying a bag of groceries. If she's not careful, she fears she could fall and break her neck, getting exactly what she deserves.

III.

And there are never really endings, happy or otherwise. Things keep going on, they overlap and blur...and there is no telling where any of them may lead.
—Erin Morgenstern

Chestnut Street

Only a few people and maybe two stray cats remember when this house was purple, not tan. Every autumn except the last, a white Maltese often frolicked through the yellow ginkgo fans confettied on the sidewalk like he was too late for a parade. A pair of wood-planked swings hanging from the giant oak out back rock themselves to sleep in the shade of the late afternoon sun. Farther up the street, close to the dead end, an infant loses her binky each day right around five o'clock. Mr. and Mrs. Miller from the yellow house on the corner sit on their porch and loudly discuss the origin of the word crocus, as she sprinkles water on hers. *It's Greek*, she shouts. *It's Hebrew*, he shouts back. *It's actually Sanskrit*, I yell, *for saffron*. They nod and wave in agreement or to encourage me to move along, I'm unsure which. The fat, pompous squirrel who's been wreaking havoc in my yard all week struts up and down the street as if taunting me with his mouth full, almost like he fears there won't be a tomorrow.

Rani Bhai

I remembered Rani Bhai the other day. The sad way I used to pray as a child for the sun to explode and drop fire like rain and burn holes in the newspaper Father read every morning instead of speaking to me.

The walk to the shore from our house wasn't easy, especially for Rani Bhai since she carried my bag and most of my belongings. I would hold her hand and skip once the shore was in sight, but she never skipped along, claiming her nubby bits jiggled too much.

"What flower would you be if you were growing on the side of Kaas Pathar, Rani Bhai," I would ask.

"The kind of flower that can heal," she would answer.

"Like what?"

"Lavender, Yarrow, Tulsi, Ajwain."

I could taste the list she sang.

Once we reached the water, she would collapse in a wooden folding chair and wrap her sari around herself. Rani Bhai napped until I was fed up with the water, and the sunshine, and the air that always smelled like rain and a history lesson. We'd snack on custard apples and roasted corn and continue our argument over who would win in a duel between Shiva and Vishnu.

After Rani Bhai was admitted to the hospital, our house became dull. Father complained about the rats in the cellar, not knowing how Rani Bhai would painstakingly apply cow pats in the corners to keep them away. No cumin wafted through the kitchen in the morning. All the music was gone.

En Route to the Happiest Place on Earth

On the last day of our family vacation, we wake up an hour late. By the time we board the shuttle bus to the amusement park, it is packed. There aren't enough seats for the three of us to sit together, so David takes Lily and they find two seats together in the back. I find a lone seat at the front of the bus and wedge myself in between another family. It's a bumpy, nausea-inducing ride as the bus skirts the artificial harbor, rocks past an endless line of souvenir shops, before coming to a stop in a long line of other vehicles waiting to pull into an available parking slot. Given it's the peak of summer, this could take a while. David and Lily are talking to each other, something funny and light that makes Lily's face brighten. I wave, trying to get their attention, but it's no use. The young son in the family next to me decides to sing. He's wearing a Mickey Mouse t-shirt and singing a song with little fart noises in it that makes his younger sister snort and giggle shamelessly. His mom snips at him, but he ignores her. After a few moments, Dad steps in, giving the kid a sharp jab with his elbow that jolts the young boy into silence and prompts him to sit ramrod straight, like a rocket awaiting liftoff. There is a faded, nearly indiscernible tattoo on Dad's forearm. Whatever it is, it has enormous, grotesque teeth.

Fur Babies

The weird religious couple next door had a hard-on for babies but couldn't have any of their own, so they ordered some from a mail catalog. Not really, but when one day the wife explained that they picked a pair of siblings from Lima who "looked so cute and perfect," I imagined them flipping through a catalog, turning their noses up at the ugly ones before finding the angelic pair they finally chose. A few months later, a delivery truck backed into their driveway, only instead of children, they got two juvenile alpacas. Everyone from the neighborhood laughed at the snafu. Kids wanted to pet them, ride on them, take selfies with them. The wife and husband didn't mind. They loved those animals as if they were human children. She knit sweater vests for them in the fall, beanies in the winter. He would walk them before and after work, took them to the vet for shots. *God had a grander plan for us. We must not fault or doubt His will. Any life given to us is a blessing,* the wife told us. And for a while, they were all very happy.

When the noise at all hours of the night became unbearable, and the lawns all over the neighborhood were eaten, shat, trampled upon, and the complaints mounted, the wife and husband were charged with negligence. Everyone from the neighborhood agreed they had been better off before they got their children. Not everyone is cut out to be a parent, after all. When the authorities raided their house to ship the beasts to a farm, everyone from the neighborhood gathered to see. The animals were found sitting quietly in their own beds wearing clean pajamas, listening to NPR, their eyes—dark pools of longing.

Funeral for a Working Girl

Bertha's ashes were in a generic plastic urn on the altar. The cross suspended behind the urn was golden smooth without the slightest stain or blemish. The preacher did the best he could with the farewell, being a complete stranger and all. He shared the few stories we had fed him, like the time Bertha took up a collection to buy Zoe's kids presents when Zoe got roughed up badly by a customer and had to be hospitalized right at Christmas, and how Bertha once gave a new girl her new pair of heels, then walked around barefoot for the rest of the night because she said it wouldn't hurt to build some character.

Halfway into the service, a man slipped in through the door and stood in the quiet shadows towards the back of the church. He stayed only a few minutes and left before we'd raised our heads following the last prayer. There were whispers that he was Bertha's estranged husband, the only member of her family to make an appearance, but we wondered. After all, much like Bertha herself, the possibilities were infinitely exotic.

Hazards of Jesting

My sister was marrying Mike, a former classmate of mine from college. Mike was a charismatic guy whose only claim to fame on campus was founding the organization, Students Against Clowns. I didn't know this about him before he fucked me in the back room of a singles mixer during our junior year. It wasn't until I saw him one afternoon, weeks after our dalliance, standing up on a table in the Student Union shouting through a megaphone about the vile nature of all things clownery, including but not limited to, court jesters, mimes, and zany pranksters. After that, I had to muster every ounce of patience just to get through a conversation with him. Then at graduation, my sister visited me, and everything changed.

"You realize he's crazy, right? I mean, Students Against Clowns? Really?" I said to her after she revealed they were dating. "I hate cabbage, but you don't see me forming a club and having the gall to use it as evidence of my social responsibility."

"Maybe you should."

"Sara, be serious."

"I am. SAC is old news. Why are you even bringing that up now? Look, I know you can't stand Mike. Maybe it's because he didn't take it any further than that one night you two had..."

"Sara!"

"But at least when he feels passionately about a cause, however impertinent it may seem to you, he does something about it. He's a great public speaker. Have you ever heard him give a speech? It's orgasmic. He has political aspirations, you know."

My sister was smitten. Beyond that, she was enthralled. Their relationship moved heavy and fast, like a stampede over my life. They went from casually dating to being engaged within a year. Before settling down they decided to embark on a three-month journey through Asia.

When they returned, the damage could not be undone. My sister was completely in love, or as I suspected, brainwashed by a potential cult leader.

One afternoon, shortly after her return, we met for lunch at a café. Sara handed me a stack of pictures from their trip just as her phone rang. Citing a work emergency, she excused herself from lunch, kissing me goodbye, and promising a longer visit next time. It wasn't until my drink arrived when I noticed she'd left the pictures on the table. I reached for my glass, knocking it over instead, drowning Sara and Mike in a bloody pool of sangria. The couple looked foolish, like two miserable idiots, as I held them up to drip dry.

Coyotes

Fearless, this pack see me again on the dirt path bypassing the tall thicket of grasses that stand on end like stubborn morning hair. They huff and puff, they snicker and snort like the vulgar boys of my youth who clung to the chain-link fence disrupting my swim meet with their "Hey babe, my vanilla needs some caramel on top" and "Hey babe, ditch the suit." But these dogs are far more cunning. They are the ruling street gang with their brindle fur and drone-worthy night vision. These dogs spurn my feckless gestures, unconfirmed prayers. They motion to each other slow and terrible, a silent lexicon unknown to me, but they don't mess with me. They let me pass. This time.

Gawker

I squint to read the tiny block letters on the stall door as I slightly lift to wipe myself. Neat penmanship, all uppercase, sure, determined strokes with a slant to the right, I WISH I WAS ANYWHERE BUT HERE. And just like that I am a witness to someone's public bathroom memoir. I stop myself from passing judgment and wonder, instead, how many other times I have become a spectator in someone else's life? Do they notice me there? What have I given testimony to? That Russian couple in front of the giant Christmas tree at Rockefeller Plaza. That's me in the upper right-hand corner, standing in my red peacoat, face upturned toward the sky away from their camera, desperately searching for a star to wish upon.

Leaving Mitzy Behind

We can see the fire from the highway. The entire hillside is ablaze. Our condo is up there somewhere. Flames claw at the night sky like an angry cat. Thick smoke blots out the stars. I don't even know how you'd begin to fight a thing like that. Maybe that's what the helicopters are for. I watch open-mouthed as they circle and dip, lights flashing in and out of the plume.

Molly is still asleep, curled up in the backseat, lightly snoring. Peter and I decide not to wake her until we're sure where we are going. The police at the roadblock don't tell us much. The wind picked up, and everything went to shit. The gymnasium of the local high school has been forced to serve as a shelter. We are to go there and wait for more information. Two more fire trucks arrive, and they pull aside the barricades to let them through.

"How bad is it really? I mean, are we going to have a home to come back to, you think?" Peter asks a cop.

The cop ignores the question and continues to wave traffic through. I back the car up and turn around to join the caravan of vehicles heading to the makeshift shelter. At the high school, a carnival was underway to raise funds for the football team. A small Ferris wheel, a merry-go-round, Whack-a-Mole, Balloon Pop, Bean Bag toss, and a few other games. People wander from game to game, booth to booth, swiping as the falling ash tickles their noses. A neon sign over the merry-go-round sputters. I can see into the gymnasium from where I park. Cots are lined up beneath posters shouting GO DRAGONS!! Two women sit at a table near the door, signing people in. A news crew is interviewing a girl who just arrived carrying a duffel bag and cardboard box full of photo frames and china. They shine an unflattering light in her face and ask about what she lost and where she'll go from here. She mumbles something about her cat, Mitzy, and having to leave her behind.

"I don't want to be here. I don't want to go in there," I say. The words just get away from me.

"Honey," Peter says. I'm afraid to open my eyes and look at him. Molly giggles in the backseat, and Peter and I turn to look at her. She reaches up to scratch her face and grins in her sleep.

A kid in a white shirt and glitter teal vest sweeps ash from the sidewalk in front of the gym's entrance. His friend juggling pins atop a unicycle near him says something funny and makes him laugh.

One mile away, everything is burning with blinding indifference.

Queen of Las Vegas

The big drunk Brit wants to know which casino George Clooney and his gang robbed in that movie. Two blocks west, I tell him. Cross the street, and you can't miss it. I top off his Guinness and tell him I'm cutting him off after that.

Marty, my once-a-week regular, is at his usual stool at the far corner. He's a talent scout. Porn, I think. He's a burly gorilla of a man with soft, sparing eyes. I tell him he'd be a more successful bouncer than scout. He agrees. I show him my new opal pendant, a gift given to me by an Australian tourist in lieu of a tip. Marty showers me with complimentary oohs and ahhs.

When my shift is over, I walk along the Strip. I'm still not drinking so I try to keep myself occupied. It's Friday night, and the tourists are out in full force. I offer to take a picture of an Italian family in front of the Bellagio fountain. I wait a beat until the music and water blast into a crescendo behind them. *Perfecto*, the dad shouts in appreciation. Souvenir shops are oozing with people and noise. There are so many lights my eyes hurt. Dizzy and dreamy, I plop down on a bus bench and smile at the passing traffic.

It stays warm out well past Thanksgiving these days, just about the only good thing about the changing climate. More warmth. You pick yourself up and go on. That's what you do. Over and over again. Sometimes happiness sneaks up on you like a lost fragment of song in the wind. Just that rare, just that precious. *Help me to grow up and be the Queen.* Vegas warms me in her bosom.

Scab

After weeks of unemployment, the temp agency set me up doing data entry and word processing for a utility gas company. The regular employees were out on strike, and every morning and evening we temps were bused through an angry picket line. The strikers spat and cursed at us as we passed, their faces contorted in abject fury like those you see in movies, or in news footage. With rumors of guns and other weapons amidst the throng, we rode most of the way bent over, chest to thighs, hugging our knees, and I wondered if this was what war felt like. Afterward the bus's windows would be glazed over with broken eggs, soda, and spit that caught the sun and sparkled almost exquisitely, like a fulsome gift from a very stingy god.

Looking for Sagittarius

The Delhi air is so polluted that the once temporary orange haze that hovered over us from dawn until dusk is now a thick plume of red, mirroring the clay dirt, blotting out nearly all the stars. Outside the city, the night is so dark, it's easy to forget which way you're going. I wish I lived out there. That one night of the big storm, awakened by sporadic flashes of blinding light, I stood out on the balcony, face upturned to the sky, grinning. Vishnu was probably taking screenshots of Earth, to show Brahma and Shiva later, and they can all share a laugh over the pathetic frailty of our momentary existence.

Now? Well, nowadays there have been more mice than people in my life. I heard on the news that mice have increased in population due to climate change. They seek the indoors where food is plentiful and reproduce repeatedly. As roommates go, they haven't been too bad. The one I usually see in the kitchen has all but claimed the wall near the range. It's fine with me, I hardly cook. Just as long as he stays away from the fridge and microwave. The gray one that haunts the hallway outside my bathroom is a little bastard. He loves scaring me at night when I get up to pee.

Some nights I wake up because I run out of air to breathe. The hollow apartment echoes like an empty jukebox and aches like my Nani's fading memory. I've tried sleeping pills, it only makes things exponentially worse.

I dyed my hair purple and gave myself a pixie cut with rusted scissors, and I think I look fabulous, but no one else seems to like it as much as I do. Most nights, I go to the rooftop to look for Sagittarius in the sky. I think if I find him, maybe I'd also find Baba, but I haven't found either of them yet. Sometimes I can hear the grandpa in the adjacent building singing Hindi love songs from the 1960s to his dead wife's picture. I think her favorites were Asha Bhosle and Mohammed Rafi.

It's almost monsoon season, it seems to come earlier and last longer with each passing year. I can taste the rain in the air as early as May. The last of the mango crop is finally ripe enough to eat. The fruit vendor sold out his cart in minutes, everyone clamoring for something good, something delicious. Maybe that's why when I cut into one, a mouse scurried away with a quarter of my mango. I bet he needed something sweet, too.

ABOUT THE AUTHOR

Renuka Raghavan is an Indian-American author who writes short-form prose and poetry. She is the author of *Out of the Blue* (Big Table Publishing, 2017) and *The Face I Desire* (Nixes Mate, 2019). Her work has been nominated for the Pushcart Prize and the Best of Small Fictions award. Look for her forthcoming work in *The South Florida Poetry Journal*, *Ruby Literary Magazine*, and *The American Journal of Poetry*. She writes and lives in Massachusetts. For a complete list of her previous publications, visit her at www.renukaraghavan.com.

www.ingramcontent.com/pod-product-compliance
Lightning Source LLC
Chambersburg PA
CBHW030347030726
47499CB00003B/943

9781950063710